A Space Family Odyssey

Lost in Space

DARTH

Library of Congress Control Number: 2024926308

ISBN: 979-8-89228-391-5   (Paperback)
ISBN: 979-8-89228-392-2   (Hardcover)
ISBN: 979-8-89228-393-9   (eBook)

Printed in the United States of America

CONTENTS

FOREWARD

As you know this story is based on the 1960's "Lost in Space" series. Here are a few pictures of that group so long ago today. This story is based on an actual family and my extrapolation of todays technology to make this story very real – especially within 100 years for the time travel at 100 times the speed of light. Making the trip to Alpha Centauri in hours instead of today's spacecraft speeds which would take several thousand years.

The idea of the PDE (pulse detonation engine)

Is the thermonuclear way of several thousand detonations per second to provide smooth acceleration to exceed the speed of light. The Graving family is the one picked out of 10,000 families – The youngest and brightest America has. It's on American adventure due to America funding the whole project to Alpha Centauri! This will be a first time firing of the greater than light hyperdrive system.

The Universe compared to our galaxy and solar system – AMAZING.

The universe is too big to even contemplate – at 13.5 billion years old and we are fairly new here. Did it start with the big bang-and where did that come from? So, lets focus on just our own galaxy – one among billions of them in the universe. We are "The Milky Way" galaxy, and our closest neighbor is the "Andromeda" galaxy at 2.22 million light years away. That means at the speed of light (186,000 miles per second or 300,000 KM per sec) it would take you 2.2 million years to reach. A LONG time. So, about our galaxy-it is a spral galaxy-there are many shapes to galaxies, but they all rotate- due to gravity. Gravity is the force of the universe that makes everything work. With out it we would just float off into space. Our galaxy is 100,000 light years across. So-what is a light year anyway? Well, let's do a little math. At 186,000 miles per sec x 3600 sec per hour x 24 hrs per day x 365 days per year, we get a huge number 5,87x10 to the 12 power, which looks like this- 587,000,000,000,000 miles or 587 trillion miles.in one year. Our closest star to our solar system is called Alpha Centauri at 4.27 light years away, that would be 4.27 x 587 trillion miles. That's a huge number and it's the closest thing outside our solar system, beyond the eight planets we know of. With our present technology, it takes us 6-8 months to get to the closest planet-Mars-the red planet. It rotates about the sun like all planets do, and it takes twice as long as Earth to orbit the sun one time. A single orbit of the sun is called an Earth year. The earth is a constant 93,000,000 or 93 million miles from the sun. This is called the habitable zone for Humans. The light and heat and gravity of the sun is just right for life! Starting with the Dinosaurs almost 1 billion years ago, life has slowly evolved here. Our telescopes and satellites into space are always looking for habitable planets – stars (suns) have planets revolving around them, and in our galaxy alone there are a trillion stars and even more planets- so many chances of life existing in our galaxy. Remember Star Wars-A long time ago, in a galaxy, far, far, away! Well that is true. We are close to the center of the universe, so that means galaxies have come and gone millions of times since we have been here. The Star Wars story has been repeated many times through the universal history of 13,5 billion years!!

Gravity – the invisible force that holds everything in the universe together! If Jupiter were to just explode and go away – our solar system would take on a whole new look. Earth would get much closer to the sun-because Jupiter is not pulling it away. We would likely burn up in a few thousand years. All the planets would move relative to each other and some might collide- causing even greater turmoil in our system. Right now, we are at total equilibrium-safe and everyday is the same. What keeps us safe were we are is the large asteroids away from us as does the sun. We are located in the perfect spot. Safety among gravity!!! Our neighbor-Mars used to be like Earth-water flowing, rivers, lakes, huge mountains, and canyons, and an atmosphere!! A living world almost 1 billion years ago-. What happened? Scientists believe that a blast from the sun emitted a solar wind so powerful – it blew away Mars' entire atmosphere, and left it like it is today-little atmosphere and no water. But-its close and has a solid surface-so that is where we go next-perhaps a manned landing in 10 years or so. A stepping stone through our solar system to other systems and life! Speaking of gravity – Mars and the moon both have 1/6th of Earth's gravity. You could hit a golf ball a mile on Mars. A new golf championship – perhaps – on Mars. The problem with Mars is that you need a spacesuit and oxygen to exist on the surface. The atmosphere is so thin. The polar ice caps might have water-or just carbon dioxide. We need water – 96% of our body is water. Another factor is that our planet is constantly being bombarded with deadly cosmic rays from our own sun and space itself. Space is a very dangerous place! You want some more numbers-cosmic radiation is in the 100-300 THZ frequency range. A hertz is one cycle per sec of movement-our TVs and radios put out HZ in smaller degrees. Your cellphone operates in the 2.4 GHZ range, that's 2.4 billion hertz. Sounds big-but really small compared to cosmic radiation-which can kill you in minutes or hours-if you have the time!!!! Our sun is a giant nuclear reactor. A fusion reactor-which means it makes energy by fusing together a hydrogen atom with a helium atom. Atoms are the smallest of all things and make up everything around you and their structure determines what it looks like and is living or dead. We are billions of atoms that makes us unique among life in the entire universe. For instance-1 pound of hydrogen fusing with 1 atom of Helium produces the energy of 10,000 tons of coal. This is the enormous energy the sun produces every thousandth of a second-a lot!!! And this fuel will keep it going for another 5 billion years-these numbers are unimaginable-yet true!!! Everytime you look up at the stars-the light you see left those stars thousands of years ago-so you are looking at the past. An alien on a distant world looking at Earth right now might see the dinosaurs!! 200 million years ago- because we are always looking into the past. When you look at the sun go down-it actually set 8.3 minutes ago, due to the distance! Mind boggling-isn't it?

We started learning about the stars several hundred years ago-when we discovered that through focusing light through a telescope into a prism, a triangular piece of glass, it showed off many colors. Turns out these colors tell us everything we need to know about a star. How far away it is, how big, how hot, how old, and its future. Now lets choose one star in the sky, Deneb. Its extremely bright-as its 1500 light years away-and yet outshines even some close planets. A huge bright star. Its always right above you-and in the summer-here it forms the summer triangle of stars-Deneb, Vega (25 light years away, and Altair-at 1.05 light years. The largest star in our part of the galaxy-Antares, would engulf our entire solar system- that is how big it is. Its 390 times the diameter of our sun with a huge radiation and gravitational field. The brightest star in the sky all year is Sirius, only 8.6 light years away-it is extremely bright and emits huge amounts of radiation-not liveable for a planet for humans!!! By the way-at our present speeds in space-it would take us 60,000 years to reach the nearest star-Alpha Centauri. We don't yet possess cryosleep-to sleep for years without aging-or warp speeds like star trek warp 9, 1000 times the speed of light-still too slow to reach most of our galaxy and we are not even at 1/10 the speed of light!!! We have a long way to go-and its up to you little guys to develop that!! GOOD LUCK., and may the force be with you.

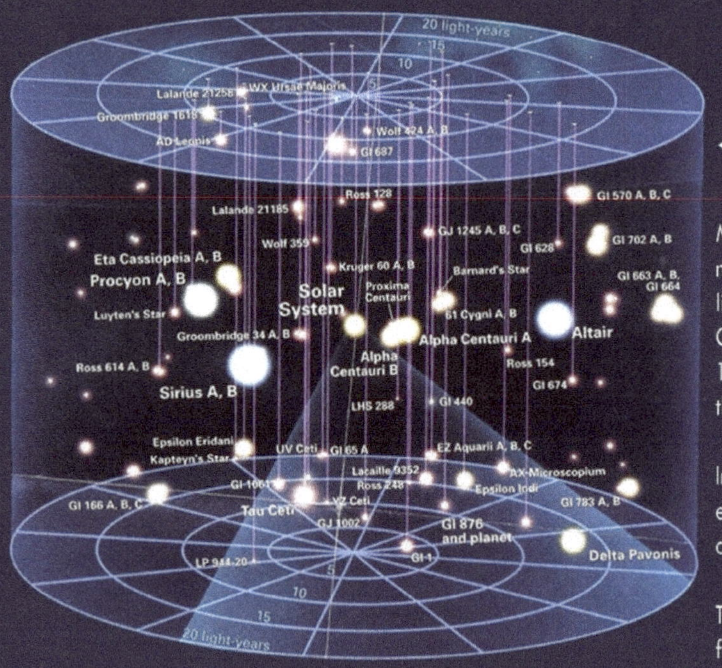

Many stars are binary or multiple. Our nearest neighbor is the Alpha Centauri triple system, 4.3 light-years away. Closest of the three Proxima Centauri (Alpha Centauri C), a red dwarf with 1/10 the mass and 1/17,000 the brightness of the sun.

In recent years astronomers have discovered evidence of planets, similar to Jupiter in mass, orbiting stars. The closest example is Gl 876.

The stars reaching 20 light-years in all direction from our sun make up the solar neighborhood. Each light year measures 5.9 trillion miles, yet the neigborhood is a tiny part of the Milky Way. Most of the Stars shown here are too dim to be seen with a naked eye, but a few, such as Sirius and Pro-cyn--- greatly exaggerated here and each actually two stars---are beacons in the sky.

In cosmic terms the sun is an ordinary yellowstar, average in size and temperature. The hottest stars glow blue, the coolest shine red.

Space Family Robinson working on robot

Space family Robinson

Penny Robinson with robot

Graving family, relaxing between training sessions

Spaceship SS Valkyrie

Adam at Pilot Station

Daisy at Control Station

Lindy with Checklist

Daisy at Engine Station

CHAPTER 1:

SPACE FAMILY Graving

T-minus 1 minute to Liftoff – first family ever in space – Mission Explore Alpha Centauri System. This was the first ever launch of a greater than speed of light velocity out of our solar system. All systems are go!

The 5 person family will be in 2 separate capsules – why we don't really know. Out of 10,000 families, this one was selected for many reasons. The ship – only tested once – was a true adventurous endeavor. It will be our first spaceflight faster than light speed – called Hyperdrive at 100 times the speed of light – requiring only 6 months. Before this it would take many years to reach. T-minus 1 minute – all is green for takeoff – the ship will take off like any jet – on with 3 different propulsion systems – normal jet with afterburns and 4 engines – system trus propulsion at 1/3 light speed until clear of our solar system. Then kick in hyperdrive. Communication will be impossible after passing Neptune.

T-30 sec – all systems GO!

Adam is uneasy – he feels like he will be responsible for anything that goes wrong. Daisy is as cool as ever. "It's no sweat guys enjoy the ride!" she yells. One final comm test between Robert and Kristen to the kids – separate modules.

The Command Module – Kids in the crew module

This was done for better survivability in case of ship break-up. Nothing had ever been tested at these speeds for so long a journey. Lindy was day-dreaming of what may lay ahead, so she was unflappable!

Robert and Kristen were making last minute checks until ignition. On ignition, the spaceship would roar down the runway jets kick-in and accelerate the ship to 1/3 the speed of light until they reach post Neptunes orbits where the light speeds hyperdrive kicks in and accelerates the ship to near 100 times the speed of light making 4.3 light year trip in just a few months. The crew would only be put to sleep for 18 hours at a time so as to conserve oxygen, water, and food intake. The ship was also equipped with 1G flight; Thanks to electromagnetic internal plating, Another first in space travel.

At ignition the ship begins accelerating down the 5 mile runway carrying the hopes and dreams of all humans on colonizing a planet in the Alpha Centuari star system. This system is a binary star cluster (2 large suns – a red dwarf sun and a large planet with atmosphere and some water and oxygen – how much we won't know till the crew land and explores. Communications will be available with Earth only til the edge of our solar system – about 3.5 billion miles. After that it will take weeks or longer to communicate.

The Graving family decided to put their names in the ring, just for the hell of it – knowing out of 10,000 highly qualified families from America only. This was strictly a US-backed venture. They would never be chosen then – that fateful day when a NASA envoy knocks on their door telling them they had been chosen. They were happy and in a state of shock at the same time. They would go through 6 months of training before liftoff, learning light speed physics, all the the ships systems, the flight plan, and emergency procedures. The kids had minimal training, but knew enough to take care of each other and love in space for a total of 9 months or so and spend as much time exploring the planet as possible. There was a crawl space between the compartments, so the family could enjoy meals and talk of how they felt things were going. It was truly a Disney World Adventure of epic-live proportions and the family was prepared – but not for what was awaiting them! They read everything about the Alpha Centauri system and the planet that they would land on. They were very excited. The flight went well til the hyperdrive kicked in and only a few months remained til touchdown. The gut dance system was very critical in every phase – just 1 degree off course after leaving our system, and they would miss Alpha Centauri completely.

All the navigation systems were critical and constantly monitored by the crew. Adam had a form group on that part. He was very adapt at math and the physics of their travel. He was the crew leader. Of course Robert was the overall mission commander and Kristen would keep the family all on track. Daisy's job was system analyst and constantly ran checks on everything from oxygen levels to food supply and Lindy was the checklist coordinator. She was very smart for her age, and seemed well adapted to this trip. After all – what could go wrong?

They had several sleep cycles approaching Mars and then a very close fly around of Jupiter – with its huge gravitational field for extra acceleration! They could all feel the speed increase – but nothing compared to hyperdrive past Neptune!

CHAPTER II:

Adam was chief engineer – making all decisions on systems and software/hardware items. Daisy does all the legwork – actually programming and wrench turning; and Lindy follows the final checklist ensuring nothing is missed. They have all had extensive simulation training and NASA has proven them ready for the voyage. Robert and Kristen are the leaders – but it's the kids that will do all the work. The spacecraft is almost ready at final engine testing commences soon. Of course, it all comes together in space where their training pays off. AS of any project of this magnitude anything can go wrong – and extensive emergency training has been accomplished on any major malfunctions.

The Kids work well together and are very excited for this opportunity. Their younger ages have nothing to do with their selection. This is a good chance to grow the future of the space program.

Adam and Daisy are very close; they are both very intelligent, outgoing, and love sports. Their dad was a running back and defensive cornerback in high school, and college, and the mother played sports as well, so that is the genetic link. They support each other in everything they do, and take good of care of little Lindy, a very close family. Their intelligence and flexibility made them all an easy choice for NASA for this mission. Adam showed a natural pilot skill set in the simulation runs, so he was chosen right off, for that, and Daisy is always happy to take on more responsibility at any time. They were very cool and calm in all their emergency procedures, simulated at NASA training facilities, and they all did very well in the centrifuge with high G-forces. Although the computer files the ship enroute, and in orbit, Adam showed intense fortitude in manipulation of the controls to put the ship anywhere it needed to be!!! Lindy, is quiet, both has an internal ferocious attitude to achieve and be just like her siblings!! A natural family. Robert and Kristen, are awesome parents, trusting their kids to attack problems and all work together-its an amazing family for this mission, and they all understand the seriousness of the perils that lie ahead, but they are prepared for any possible dangers. A good choice for NASA!!

CHAPTER III:

A little bit on the engine systems of the spacecraft – named after its designer – Darth I and therefore called the Darth II. It has 3 different drive modes. Sublight for manoeuvring in any solar systems and planet approaches and departures. The second drive takes the ship to about 0.9 speed of light and the star drive or hyperdrive up to (theoretically 100 times speed of light). Daisy is the engine monitor and local expert! She shows exuberance and a love for Engine system and speed. Yes, she is a speed freak!

Daisy at Engine Monitor Station

CHAPTER IV:

T-minus 5 sec. Ignition – The roll down the runway is quick – as they rotate directly into the vertical. They pass the speed of sound (about 660 knots) at only 5000 feet. The crew has experienced this acceleration in the centrifuge – but this is real – with no emergency stop button. The crew is in monitor mode til they reach 1/10 the speed of light. Then checklist are run much conversation between crew commander and the kids. Mars approaches fast and they get to see an actual interplanetary fly-by not simulation – everyone is excited and suddenly a crash and warning lights go off everywhere. The ship hit an asteroid and lost all external communication. Everyone is busy at their jobs – accessing damages and luckily no leaks. Adam is monitoring as Daisy seals off inner dull damage and keeps the ship

Robert and Kristen's Command Center

on course. The crew is working well together now! The damage is light – but someone – probably Robert – will have to go cut and take a look for external damage – his first real spacewalk! Kristen is checking each crew member for any damage and reassuring them! Bitchin Betty, the ships computer voice with AI is telling everyone their options and how things are going. The computer system is the most sophisticated ever built for space. Also Betty monitors all crew physical characteristics and oxygen levels! Very important on this trip – any external

O2 leaks could spell an abort and return to Earth. Robert is outside monitoring the hull and has a wonderful view of Jupiter!

Navigation hollogram

The hull is intact and Robert re-enters the craft. The crew settles in for a good meal and conversation on the near disaster before retiring to sleep. Their sleep chambers are all in separate quarters and on injection pats them right to sleep. They dream but never move as their bodies are reduced to 5 heart bpm and respiration to 3. They are in a very deep sleep. Not cryosleep or time sleep but similar to reptilian behavior – a crocodile can hold its breath for hours at the waters edge awaiting prey. The crew sleep is similar to this. Like bear hibernation!

Crew Quarters

Robert and Kristin's Command Quarters

CHAPTER V:

The crew awakes – it takes a while to recover from that deep sleep! Just a few minutes, a drink of (yes – just Gatorade) to replenish all the electrolytes and boost energy is taken in. Lemon-Lime seems to be the favorite! They orbit past Jupiter and tell mission control all about their close encounter – all is a go. As Lindy runs the crew checks and systems checks Betty – tells them to 2 days to hyperspace – everyone is very excited! No human has ever reached this far! Adam is still feeling like he should do more for crew safety and efficiency – all normal at this point! The crew is well prepared; however they still practice emergency procedures several hours a day! It's real for Robert and Kristen – but its fun for the kids!

Another 18 hours of sleep and they pass Neptune – preparing for hyperdrive! Everyone is very excited. No human has ever exceeded light speed so this will be amazing. According to Einstein, it's never been done and can't be! The crew will soon find out! It's like the "Trinity Test" in 1945. The first atomic bomb test – would it destroy the world or be about 12 kilotons – as predicted! It was as predicated in this case we don't have a true prediction. The kids don't give it much thought – but Robert and Kristen are very concerned – where will they emerge?

First Atomic Bomb Test

Alpha Centauri is a binary system – 2 suns – similar to our own, a red dwarf star (already died out – but of no consequence – and their target Centauri B – The planet – similar in mass and space to Earth – but we have never seen through its atmosphere! This is the key – the atmosphere must screen out a lot of cosmic radiation and have oxygen and water! That's asking a lot!

That is the target – once hyperdrive is initiated who knows what will really happen except instead of 4 years at the speed of light you will reach the system (Alpha Centauri) in 1/100 of that or .0425 years which is pretty neat eh! A few skep cycles and you are there.

* All this depends on the computer – if it doesn't cut out of hyperdrive into sublight speed you could overshoot the system by so many days or if you actually travel in the wrong direction you will have no point of reference and be "Lost in Space"! Not a good thing – you would also not know where Earth is or how to get there.

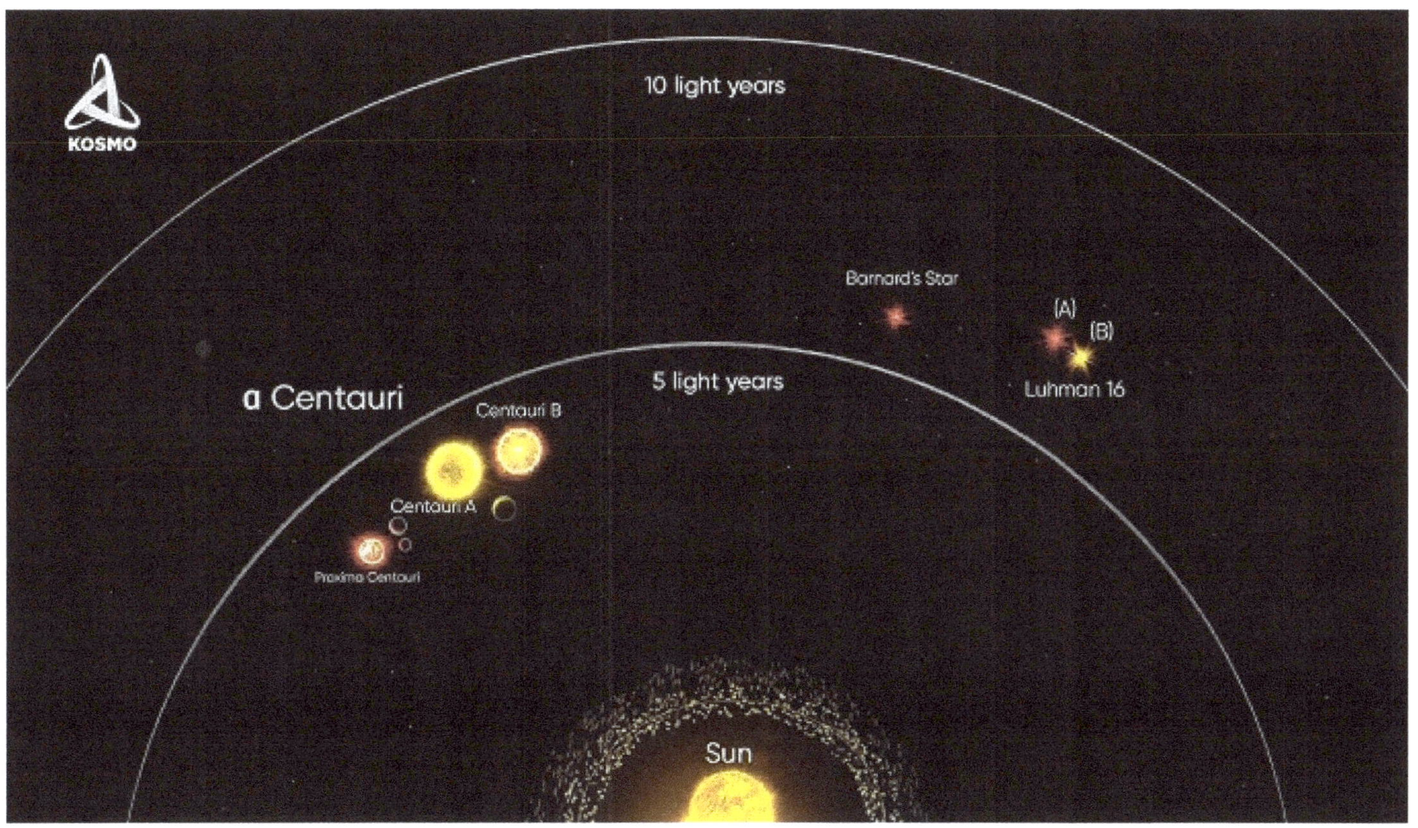

Alpha Centauri

CHAPTER VI:

T-minus 1 hour to hyperdrive traveling to 0.9 speed of light past Neptune. Robert will give the command to Adam to initiate hyperdrive! Daisy will coordinate all spacecraft systems for the inversed velocity and Lindy will monitor all checklists for any malfunctions which Betty – the computer will tell the crew with a countdown. T-Minus 1 minute lose – No abort now – Betty tells the crew the navigation system just dropped off line – no turning back now – and whoosh – with an acceleration of 12 G's for 15 sec. The spacecraft starts its acceleration. Robert knows as does Adam that now they have no directional control or hyperdrive shutdown! This is a worst possible case. Betty gets off on emergency broadcast to Earth of the malfunction as the spacecraft is now in the ort cloud between systems! The crew can only wait and hope for the best!

CHAPTER VII:

The hyperdrive shuts down to sublight speed and there is nothing there . "Betty" tells the crew to evaluate known positions off any stars in the vicinity. They are all far away and no Alpha Centauri. The worst case has happened – between their star charts and Betty – the computer there is dead silence. "Where the hell are we screams everyone in unison. They check the hyperdrive it is – inop and it shut down much later than predicted!

They figure they are at least 5 light years too far. Without hyperdrive – they can't go anywhere at 0.9 speed of light and they have no computer control for direction. Everyone is in panic mode. Robert decides to hold present position with all engines shut-down and have a family meeting. "Betty" has little input except they have no way of knowing any direction to travel.

Robert tells the family: "We only have enough O2 (oxygen) for 24 hours. Food and water for 7 days – but that won't matter with no O2! Ok; Kristen – any navigational news? Kristen hesitates; well with no known stars to navigate by – we have no reference points; so we have no direction and at 0.9 c (.9 speed of light) it wouldn't matter anyway". Adam anything from the crew – Daisy pops right up as usual. The sensors are rolling and I'm picking up a system only.3 light years away – one star and several planets – all 3 planets have atmospheres – "Great says Robert" we can make it with time to spare – its definitely not Alpha Centauri, but we have little choice at this point. Kristen – pick up the sensor feed and lets head for that system – as we get closer we will gather more information on the three planets." Lindy calmly says – "well – what if none of them have any O2 or water or are too hot or cold?" Kristen – ETA to system – "about 3.4 hours", OK, everyone prepare your stations – First we scan each planet and pick out the best one. Unfortunately, once we are landed – that's it – no power or O2 to blast off again– we must make the right decision! The crew is calm and knows the risks as they man their stations. The Sun is similar to Earth's a Red giant – about 3 billions yrs old with 3 planets

– as they get closer the inner planet is too hot – over 800°F and the other is too cold and not enough atmosphere – The middle planet is it. Some O2 is detected – a thick atmosphere with mountains and canyons but they won't know about O2 levels or temp or vegetation til after landing – They never trained for this!

Daisy at Control Station – After time travel

Lindy at Station in Battle gear

Lindy is busy with checklist for approach and landing – Robert will coordinate the entire approach – Adam is designated pilot – so he will land the craft – they don't know if the vertical landing stabilization will function so another guess. The atmosphere is a bit thicker than Earth – Nitrogen and oxygen have been detected; This is so good. Everyone crosses their fingers as they hit the atmosphere. The stabilizers are working, so; it is a smooth entry – no sign of the surface yet. All of a sudden the crew gasps. The surface – a lake of hopefully water – readings from the sensor array show 18% oxygen and 80% Nitrogen – almost identical to Earth!

The Valkryie over the Planet Surface

Adam yells "Standby for vertical mode – a flat piece of land looms. There is vegetation and maybe water. They appear to have hit the astronomical jackpot!" Adam rolls a smooth landing and they shut down all engines and check the sensor array. Before exiting the craft, they need to know, temperature O2 levels, cosmic radiation, water vapor in the air, lots of data. So, Robert decides to have a crew meal to say a prayer for a safe landing. Even though they don't know where they are. The sensor data will be ready soon, so they all settle down for a nice meal – The food processors on the ship is excellent at making anything taste the way you want it – with all the nutrients required for a healthy diet. Lemonade for a drink and Kristen puts on some soothing music – The family is happy and very optimistic!

Crew Dinning Facility

The Family's new planet with lots of water

Even at their younger ages – These astronauts are performing at high efficiency levels and everyone knows their job. "Betty" comes over the intercom with good news – the soil is rich and soft. There is vegetation all around – plants, tress and the lakes are actually water H2O!

The air is breathable and a warm 78-degree F air temp. Luck is definitely on their side – this may not be Alpha Centauri – but it couldn't be any better than this! Everyone is very happy and excited. This one thing they don't know is – are any living intelligent organisms here.

No structures of any kind – the planet is younger than Earth – about 2 billion years old – less than half of Earth.

As the crew prepares for a new day out on this new planet; Robert exclaims, "WOW ;we all look so different-every body look at each other-its's a sif the short time travel aged us years ,some more than others, and their NASA flight suits even changed to different suits. There is no explanation for this ,I guess part of Einstein's theories were correct-things have changed, but we are in good shape,every one feel OK?" They look at each other as if seeing one another for the first time, but they like it! They aged between 2,and 7years or so. They decide to let NASA in on it later as they prepare to exit the spacecraft and explore their new world.SO, apparently ,just exceeding the speed of light even for a short time will change you ,but how much, and will they return to their former selves if they try it again, or age even more ,again; no answers for all their questions, but ,everyday appears will hold new and exciting adventures on this strange, but beautiful world, they now call home!

Now the big question – what to wear and who goes out first. Robert decides – he will lead and Adam and Daisy will accompany him. They will not wear spacesuits and will carry pulse rifles – for defense only – sensors did not show any life as we know it. They enter the airlock – Kristen is in charge of the ship now. They will make a sweep for the ship for damage then use their sensing device to test the air, water, and vegetation. Standby to open outer door! Mans first step on another world! As the door opens – a fresh breeze of sweet smelling air greets them – they all take readings before checking the ship – the small lake is indeed water – just like Earth – The vegetation is soft and green and has a sweet odor. The soil will be analysed later; so Robert gives the command to check the ship. Its quite evident where the asteroid hit them; but no internal damage – they were very lucky there!

"Ok guys, that's it for this trip outside, let's get all the computer systems up and running – Adam – full engine check – find out what we need to do to get the hyperdrive back online. Use "Betty" – keep me noted!" " Ok – crew meeting in 5 minutes. Everyone is very excited – it's like their own personal Disneyland.

As Robert addresses the crew; "Ok everybody – so far we have been extremely lucky – we are on a Earth-type planet. Breathable air, water, vegetation, nice balmy temp, good atmosphere, we have a lot of data to digest before we know how hospitable our new home is. No clouds out – might be a clear night for some star mapping and getting. We have a lot to learn about our new world; but lets bow our heads and be thankful that we were resourceful enough to get this far. After a few nights of star-charting – we might even figure out where we are! "Lindy – keep us updated on everything we are doing and make new checklists accordingly. Adam – your own engine mech – so figure that out and keep Daisy opposed of all systems. Your mom and I will coordinate supplies and a plan for future outings. I think a celebration is in order. We are all on, have food, water, and O2 – all the things we were hoping for. Well done so far – let's have a big meal, good conversation, and some music tonight we will see what temperatures to expect and other atmospheric conditions. The ship is intact; so we shouldn't need any defuse systems to set up. Look forward to a beautiful day tomorrow and more findings – we will stay close to the ship til we know more about our surroundings. Any questions?

Lets all have a great night and Kristen will have a wonderful breakfast prepared. We have to figure out a time schedule since we don't know how long a day is here. Everyone be thinking of a name for our new planet; which apparently no human has ever seen before. We will set a comm system tomorrow and start transmitting data to anyone who might be listening." Daisy says, But what if they are hostile?" she is always the inquisitive one! Robert answers – we will take that as it comes – but we have to relay to NASA somehow – it's a question of power! Daisy – that's your area! Daisy says, "Great – open my big mouth and I have to do all the work!" Robert answers. "Well, you asked for it!" – Everyone laughs and goes to bed – their cubicles are programmed for an 8 hour sleep. The ships environmental control are on automatic – about the 72°F. "Just right! And a good night to the Graving family – Lost in Space – and loving it!

Ship name: SS Valkyrie

*Next decision – get computer online Day 2

Day 2 was sunny and warm again, the sun was high in the sky – so today the crew will not a day length and temperature scale and of course – the morning meeting! Robert addresses the

---

1 are there animals here – we haven't seen any birds.

crew (family) – Did everyone sleep good?" The crew is rested and ready to explore! But first important matters for immediate action. "Our first problem is the computer. Without that we cant find where we are or navigate off this planet. Although, this is a very nice planet (I would recommend to NASA for this planet for colonization)." Daisy knows what they have to do and can't wait to tell the crew the bad news. Robert, "Ok Daisy – what systems do we have and what can we do?" Daisy is anxious, but ready; "First we have environmental control and the sensor array works, but we have no computer!" Robert knows what that means, Daisy, "The only way to get the computer back is a total reboot of the entire system. It will take an hour and are losing everything. The emergency DC and AC busses on the batteries are all we have! If the reboot fails – we are left with only the Batteries and emergency busses – no sensors – no atmospheric control – not much. The Batteries will be Ok – with solar power to constantly recharge – but we will be stuck here permanently!" Kristen says – The good news is – the food processors will be functional!" Robert – "So – we don't have a lot of chances – we try to reboot and get the computer back or we are stuck here forever! Adam say "Without the computer – we cannot get the hyperdrive back on line, so – we can't navigate or go anywhere at sublight speeds." Ok, says Robert – lets take a vote. We either try a reboot or we are here for a long time. Is there anything we have overlooked?" The crew is quiet – they all know what this means. "Ok – then I say we try the reboot – the only good news is we have O2, water, food, and a good temperature. The computer system seems to work. There is N and S pole on this planet – so we can navigate around in the rover and check out more of the planet.

The Rover – "Centauri"

So – I recommend we all go outside get the rover out and discover – and start the reboot?" Questions? We aren't sure but the atmosphere probably shields us from most of the cosmic radiation. Wear your suits – core most skin – just in case. Ok – Daisy – let us know when you're ready to reset. Everyone drink lots of water – stay hydrated and lets hope for the best! Ok – let's go – everyone stay close to the ship as Daisy and I use the rover to check the local area. Ok – that's the plan for now. Questions?" Kristen, Adam, and Lindy scrounge around for animal life and the crew is ready for the reset! They have been lucky so far – so – here we go. "Daisy hit the reset! The ship goes down as everything drops off line. Now – they can only wait! Ok – let's deploy as briefed! No-one alone and stay in sight of the ship at all times. Daisy – coordinate with Lindy on everything you do. ; "but Dad, she doesn't matter" – Robert "she coordinates and logs in everything – very important. Just relax and enjoy this little adventure – remember – there are living creatures here – we just haven't seen them yet! Daisy – ok Dad – let's get it on!

Daisy in Combat gear

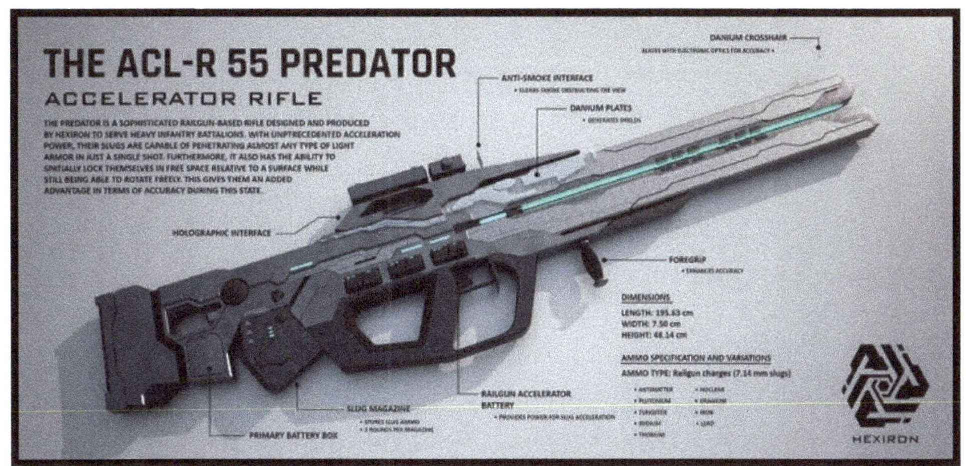

The Plasma Rifle

DAY 2 Evening:

Robert – Ok Daisy – it's about that time – lets head back and see about the reboot!" Daisy – "Ok – but Dad – what if it doesn't work -?" – "Ok Lets take things one at a time – we have plenty of time – Meanwhile – at the ship – everyone is waiting as the Rover arrives – "Ok – this is it – Daisy – let her rip! Daisy – Ok – but this is my best guess – so don't blame me if it doesn't work!" – Robert – "Daisy – Reset Now!" As Daisy hits the reset button – nothing happens! – Daisy – "Crap, I knew we missed something – Lindy – what did we miss?" Lindy – (who seldom speaks – only acts – "We missed nothing – checklists was perfect hit it again!" – Daisy "Ok- here we go"

Daisy presses the reset button again and after a flash of light – nothing! "Ok, says Robert – let's wait a few minutes – let the trons do their thing!

Everything dies again! – "Ok – don't panic" – electricity can be a strange bed-fellow – maybe if we reverse the polarity of the system – that may work." Daisy – "Ok – give me a minute and we will try it again – but we could blow all the circuits –" Robert – "It's the only choice Daisy. Do it! Daisy follows Lindy's checklist for reverse polarity and Daisy hits the reset – Wham – a huge light and shaking as the whole ship is about to explode -; Daisy – "Its Ok – that's normal – wait a few moments" – Wow – as the crew looks on the whole ship lights up and the sound of engines running – "We did it – it worked – We are back in business!" Robert "Ok – everyone man your stations and Lindy run the checklist for every system! It's a true miracle – all systems are back on line – even the hyperdrive and computer! What a relief – just – lets figure the computer for where we are and where Earth and Alpha Centauri are! They were almost 8 light years off course. Ok – Lets let the computer configure all systems and have a lunch briefing! Everyone is so relieved – they feel like they are in control again!

DAY 3 After a good nights sleep and the computer controlling navigation – they have breakfast and decide activities for the day!

CHAPTER VIII:

A NEW BEGINNING

The computer is up and running – all checks Ok! According to the computer; they are orbiting the star 61 Cygni; which is pretty far from Alpha Centuari. They are about 10 light years away from where they are supposed to be. Now the computer is checking the hyperdrive for its capability. Family meeting time! Robert says "Well – we are about twice as far out as we are supposed to be. If the hyperdrive doesn't work at 100%; It could be a long flight to Alpha Centauri. Adam and Daisy – monitor the engine systems, Kristen and I will take the rover and check out some more of the planet. Lets have a comm-check every 30 minutes. Lindy make sure you follow the procedures. Everyone stay in the ship until we find some animal life in the area. There's water – good temperature, and vegetation – there has to be life! "Ok Lets do it!" Robert and Kristen head due south until they find something. The computer is working hard on getting the hyperdrive up and running. Until all checks are a GO – they they wont know if they can takeoff or not. The sky is an Earth like blue and a slight breeze with the smell of flowers in the air.

CHAPTER IX:

DAY 3

About 5 miles south Robert and Kristen climb a steep slow and crest overlooking a valley. "Wow, says Robert, look at that, its like the dinosaurs! There are a group of at least 100 herbivores strong in the 3' to 10' range and grazing on the grasses. Its like we are on Earth 100 million years ago!" Kristen says – well where there are herbivores – there have to be carnivores. I think we should go very slow from here with pulse rifles ready! Robert agrees and they circle the valley on the rim. The animals seem oblivious to their presence. Well - we could kill one and have some real meat for a change – about that time – they all split running – and Robert sees why – a Lion-sized carnivore running and grabbing one of the herbivores – it has spikes on its back and large fangs – they need to be careful – it appears to be a skilful hunter! I think we need to take some video and head back to the ship. No comm with the kids – something maybe wrong.

Herbivores grazing in Valley

Our Planet Carnivore Raptors

Daisy is switching systems to get comm for NASA transmission and Adam is monitoring the hyperdrive auto – reset. Daisy complies. Adam says "Hey we need a comm check with mom and dad now – don't reset yet.", "Adam to Dad on Freq Channel 1 – come in!" Dad hears him and reports they are on the way back new video. Hows the reset?" Adam – "We had to hold off to communicate with you!" – Dad replies – "Ok we are almost back go ahead and do the reset and get the big comm antenna out, so we can start to power up the transmission system to get off a call to NASA; although it will take about 10 hrs to get an answer!" Adam – "Ok – Dad pulling out the gear and Daisy is starting a reset." Ok – see you soon – out!

They can communicate with Earth because of subspace frequency modulation which – with enough power will allow a transmission at much greater than light speed. But the antenna array has to be perfect and without accurate directional control – who knows? With their star charts and the computer (check the diagram) there are several more suns only a few light years away. But for now – they are happy where they are.

CHAPTER X:

Communication

Ne of their other problems is the sun Cigni-61 they orbit. It has considerable gravitational force and any engine problems after Tlo and they may not be able to pull away. The universal law at gravitation states the force $F = G\, m_1\, m_2/\, r^2$ where m1 is the mass of their ship (in this case in Kg, and m2 is the mass of the sun and r is the distance from the center of the sun to their ship. The computer has calculated they are 88 million miles from the sun, G is the universal gravitational constant measured at 6.67×10^{-11} N-m^2/Kg^2; where N (Newton is the force acting on the ship. 1 Newton = 4.45 lbp (pound force)

So; Adam – using the computer has figured out that their ship weighs = 25 tons with fuel and water, O2, etc – the sun Cigea61 is 1.8×10^{28} Kg and the distance of 88 million miles in meters is 1 mile = 1610 meters ; the r = 1.4×10 meters

Plug it all in and the F from the sun getting on their ship in planet orbit would be F = 6.67 x 10^-11 N – m^2/Kg^2 (25,000 Kg x 1.8 x 10^28 Kg)/(1.4 x 10^11m)^2 = 4.5 x 10^32 (1.4x10 reducing – we get 6.67x10^-11 N-m^2/Kg^2 (4.5 x 10^32 kg)^2/(1.4x10^11 m)^2

This is why a computer needs to do this; but by using basic algebra and knocking out the Kg, and m, leaves you with the answer your ship is being subjected to 21.4 x 10^10 N of force or 95x10^10 pounds of force. As you can see – the distance has a greater effect on the ship than the masses of each body; so the ship can easily escape 95x10^10 pounds of force since the engines even in sublight put out about twice that force: but as you get closer to the sun the distance is squared; so the force will be times 4 the closer you get. Almost the same as Earth. This planet has a 8.8 m/s^2 acceleration due to gravity – so they will need about 15,500 miles per hour of escape velocity – the sublight engines can easily get them out of orbit and on their way – no hyperdrive needed – but to get to any other system – they will the need the hyperdrive for even 2 light years – a difference of a few months vs years. Once they are in space any hyperdrive real function will leave them; bit floating or crawling thru space to reach a planet or any sun – and they may not have any planets. So – once again – they must have the computer and hyperdrive to go anywhere! Same old pattern. Dad tells Daisy to compute everything so if they lose the computer again they can navigate with coordinates the computer gives them before takeoff. But that is weeks away. They need to develop a hydropower garden for fresh vegetables and they can kill a herbivore for fresh meat. There seem to be many of them around. But where will they go; Alpha Centauri b (the planet they were first headed for could not be any better than where they are. The computer has determined a year here is very close to Earth – about 400 days and very little planet tilt – so not much change in seasons. They will gladly take a year-round average of 70-80°F. If they can grow vegetables – they will be happy. Robert tells Kristen and Lindy to work on the hydroponic garden. About 100ft square – they have seed and water. No problem there – the soil has been analyzed as Earthlike – very fertile with lots of minerals.

About (they figure a day is 23 hrs. again – Earthlike – around 3 pm the sky clouds over and something like hail starts to fall – only it isn't ice – its rock-like – a meteor shower. Robert yells – "Everyone in the ship and lock down" the shower increases for about an hour – very small rocks. No damage they can see – but you wouldn't want to be out in it. How often does this happen? Not a big deal but it could be frequent. Daisy has the coordinates plotted for manual navigation to either Alpha Centauri – or Earth – just a few months travel. The Antenna rigging seems intact – so they divert power to communications and send Earth a message on a special NASA frequency just for their ship. Robert decides to launch a communications satellite to about 20,000 km to reach Earth! This will give them constant communications. Should take about 10-12 hours for a response. They want to know what NASA thinks about staying where they are or taking off. There won't be any rescue ship; as theirs is a one of a kind in cost and system development! The crew agrees to further explore this planet although smaller than Earth – it has lots of canyons – smaller mountains, and lakes and vegetation everywhere. They also want to find more animal life. Tomorrow Robert and Daisy will take the rover – which they aptly named; "Centauri" since that's where they are supposed to be. This time they will go much further south and see what lies beyond the valley. So, late moving on Day 4 on their planet - Robert and Daisy head across the valley – no animals like Robert and Kristen saw a few days ago. Lots of vegetation and on the other side of the valley, they encounter a huge and deep canyon, no way across or around. This one, they get out of the Centauri once check the plants. A wide variety of lush plant life. Daisy touches a few and Robert takes some samples to take back and analyze. They get back into the rover and Daisy notices some redness on her hands and starts to feel a little queasy! She tells Robert she doesn't feel good. The red blotches spread and she feels hot and heavy! Robert says they will hurry back – contacts the ship and tells them to ready the Med-Lab for Daisy; They arrive at the shop – Robert carries Daisy to the Med-Lab and lays her on the computerized table and asks "Betty" to analyze. He also has the plants checked. Daisy has a high temperature and is covered in red areas covering most of her skin. "Betty" detects a foreign substance in her blood and tells the crew she will inject Daisy with an antibiotic and fever reducer. Obviously she touched a poisonous plant. The computer is analyzing the plant and finds a substance that is indeed poisonous to humans. Of course, the animals know which plants to eat and which to avoid. The crew has dinner and awaits an update on Daisy. Robert tells everyone – wear gloves to handle any vegetation until they know which ones are safe. Daisy's temp is reducing and the antibiotics is working. Thank God – "Betty" and the computer are working at 100%. The sun is setting so everyone will rack early tonight while Daisy recovers!

DAY 5:

North Pole Area

Daisy awakens – the temp is gone – the red blotches are gone and she feels great – thank God for the Med-Lab and computer – and of course "Betty"!

The crew is considering a rover trip to the poles – North to avoid the big canyon – the rover has navigational and radar systems to detect terrain ahead. They will close up the ship – and all head north for a look at the pole. Assuming this planet even has a pole. Its probably a few days trip each way, so the pack provisions and weapons – you never know! About 400km north mountains loom and the temp drops – they may be close. The radar shows a gap in the mountains and so they head for that. Still with this atmosphere and temp – they have seen no birds for an Earthlike planet. This is very unusual. The temp is dropping as they pass the mountains – down for their camp 75°F to the 40s now. They have a good heater in the rover and good warm space suits! Robert figures another day and they should see the ice cap! Something swoops down out of nowhere and now they know – these are not birds; but the size of the rover and huge wings and big teeth – they are envious as to what these are.

North Pole Ice Dragon

They look like dragons! They hit the snow and temp is down below water freezing level at 32 F! The crew decided to use American Standard measures – like miles and Fahrenheit in degrees as they are more used to it. The rover batteries are doing nicely; and Robert figures their satellite is about in range for a NASA reception to their earlier message. Adam takes over driving the rover – Robert takes a nap, Daisy is on the communications and Lindy – of course is writing a ledger and checking procedures. Another huge dragon appears – they are in snow now – about 20°F and they decide to call their new friends – "Ice Dragons" – they are eating. The birds most likely and stay near the poles.

Flash – Daisy has a comm link with NASA. This could be good or bad! They don't want to go to Proxina B (Alpha Centauri); because its an unknown. Any malfunctions and they die there. NOT GOOD!

About that time, an Ice Dragon lands right in front of the ship – its as big as the rover and huge fangs and wings with clawed feet. Thank God they stay at the polar caps. Robert decides to drill to see how thick the caps are and get samples from below – that will tell them a lot about the geology of the planet poles. The comm from NASA is coming in and here is the jist of their conversation. NASA understands their situation and how they got where they did. The hyperdrive was new and totally untested. They can't afford to get lost any further. So, NASA agrees explore the planet – get as much info as possible and keep NASA appraised of any new developments. Good news! They like where they are and will continue to explore the entire planet for clues of any intelligent life – you never know!

CHAPTER XI:

The family is happy and now they will launch a GPS tracking satellite and the another one for full planet coverage! Things are really looking up! Lindy logs in the NASA comm and everyone takes a well-deserved rest! They have the samples for computer analyzation and head back to the ship. Its evening now and the days all seem to be about the same. Newer many clouds and the atmosphere has been analyzed to screen out all harmful radiation and burning rays! A true paradise so far. Daisy is asleep at the system's station, Adam is driving the rover and Mom and Dad are talking over what and where to go next! A few hours and back home. Yes, it seems like their home already and the need to explore that canyon more with a river at the bottom – maybe even some fish. The flock of birds is quite putting.

DAY 6: CARNIVORES

The whole family leaves today to cross the canyon and check the southern hemisphere. The Rover has rockets and hug wheel impact absorption ability – they could jump part of the canyon – if necessary. They turn east and plot waypoints from their 2 orbiting GPS satellites the put in 10,000 mile orbits yesterday – they are working great. So as they head east about 30 miles – the rover can easily exceed 65 miles per hour if flat terrain. The canyon narrows, and this is where they will jump. Robert orders, "Lindy – procedures for jump – everyone strap-in tight as they have never done this before. The rocket boosters are a go. They have ½ mile to accelerate to 60 mph jump speed. Ok – throttles up – Adam you have the controls – Go! They hit the edge and rockets fire after and down. The canyon is beautiful – much like the Grand Canyon on Earth. They easily hit the other side – a few bounces and they are safe. Robert orders everyone out to inspect the rover! All is well – Lindy logs it in and they continue – just as they power up – wham – something hits them from the side – a much larger ones are on this side of the canyon. Its as big as an elephant and as ferocious! Its carnivores and wonders off!

They continue to discover more mountains ahead. Nothing uncrossable; however! Daisy spots a cave entrance on ground radar – so – its off to explore – this, they will never forget!

A huge cave opening that goes quite deep and down about 15°, Robert has Kristen and Adam remain with the ship. "Ok, everybody wear night vision and a plasma rifle – we know large carnivores are here and this could be their den!" They proceed inside – its damp and wet – a little cooler than outside – they progress about ¼ miles – no comm with the ship – probably interference from the cave. They take rock samples and then Daisy yells out – "over here now!" laying by against the rock looks to be a skeleton in a suit of the same kind – the head is mostly intact but nothing like a human head – they decide to move the whole skeleton with stretcher – back to the ship. Kristen says, "Wow! Just what we have been looking for – signs of intelligent life!" Robert, "Ok – don't jump to conclusions – let's take it back to the ship – go thru decontamination, and put it in Med-Lab for "Betty" to analyze, agreed?" Ok – everyone is excited. Its in the galaxy and close to Earth – geologically speaking of course! The hydroponic garden is working well for fruits and vegetables – but they need real protein – not synthesized. Robert decides he and Adam will hunt for a herbivore tomorrow analyze it and have a real "human" dinner tomorrow night! It's late – "Betty" will scan the creature all night and hopefully tomorrow – some answers!

Cave entrance with Alien inside

Alien found in cave

DAY 7: Everyone awakens and "Betty" has a report – the skeleton and head structure are about 120 million years old! "WOW" says the crew – the Jurassic period of dinosaurs on Earth! It appears to be telepathic – since no sign of vocal clouds or jaw movement for speech. The head and brain are larger than ours – so reaches great intelligence – but what happened to them and where are more – was the cave a refuge from carnivores or a home. 120 million years ago is a long time to be just "hanging around".

Robert has other concerns; Never a cloud in the sky and yet lakes and rivers everywhere – an underground H2O source perhaps. There has to be a ship or other creatures on the planet somewhere. "Betty" says the computer analyzed all data and this planet was not their home. They came from somewhere else but where?

CHAPTER XII:

They take the rover south over the canyon its beautiful scenery everywhere. No carnivores, Robert thinks they are curious, but will not attack. Such strange looking machines and a group of people – plus they have the pulse rifles!

Family overlooking valley to the South

Family cruising through valley canyon

20-30 miles south they find another cave – much larger and deeper. As they all explore – Adam finds the leftovers of a crashed ship. There are 2 skeleton fossils of aliens in spacesuits in the cave. They have been there a long time. They need to get this back at the ship for computer analysis. The other alien was over 100 million years old. Intelligent creatures get within 20 light years of Earth then, so where did they come from? What killed them? And did they find Earth?

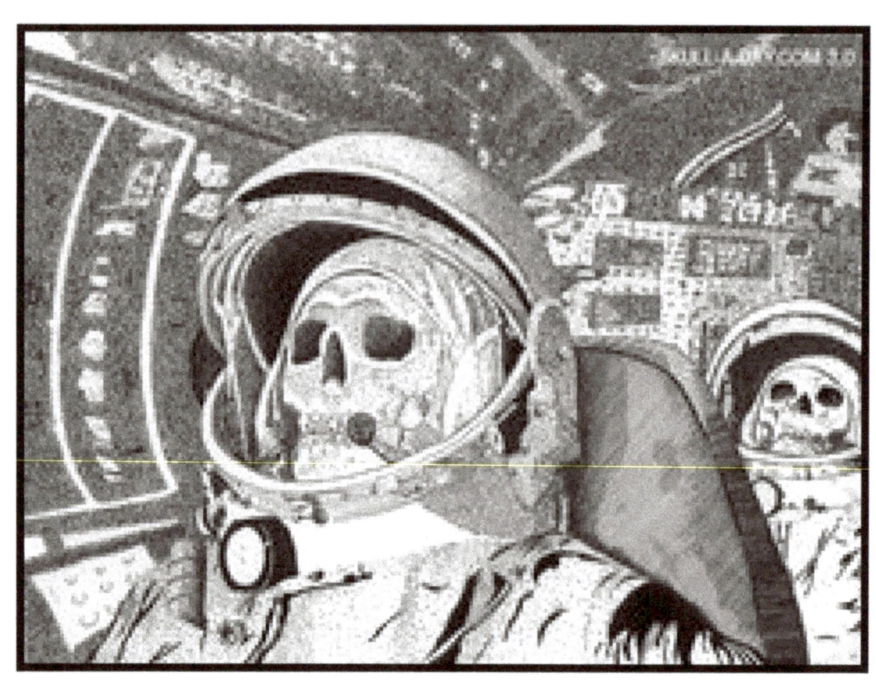

Alien in crashed spacecraft

Alien in wreckage

Hopes the carnivore was satisfied with its kill. They drive to the kill and load it on the rover – the ship's computer will tell them if its fit for human consumption. As they leave the area – the carnivore eyes them as it feasts on its kill with great curiosity! Back at the ship, everyone is excited – the computer in Med-Lab has a report.

WOW! DAY 9, only on this planet and they have discovered so much! Meat – for the table – the computer says only cook minimum medium – well done and drink lots of planet water! Everyone is so excited – its like "The Last Supper of Christ" – only its their first real meal from the flesh of another planet! WOW.

"Betty" has much to report and they are all in awe! "Betty" reports – these new alien fossils were only 1.2 million years old and not related at all to the earlier much older fossils they found in the other cave. Why in an oxygen environment these aliens fossilized and didn't decompose. Also – evidence shows that our early DNA is related to the latest alien ship crew they found – did we come from them – interesting ideas as we continue to research who and what they are and did this planet have an atmosphere over 100 million years ago? Still looking for answers as we explore this beautiful, strange world!

CHAPTER XIII:

DAY 9

nly 9 days here and we love this planet – the computer says the herbivore meat is Ok and we cook out tonight at sunset. Veggies and real meat from a beautiful planet – will send NASA another update later. Did we come from these intelligent space-faring creatures and where did they come from – many questions to answer! The meal is ready – Kristen and I will share a cabernet tonight and celebrate our newfound knowledge of our galaxy. It is so huge its unimaginable! We cook and eat – Daisy says, "Um – taste like chicken! We all laugh and feast on our good fortune, we are at home!

The computer found a match for the herbivores on this planet – the Stegoceras Validum – lived on Earth 72 million years ago and an exact DNA match. The plot thickens. What is the connection between this planet and Earth? They are almost identical in every way today and 72 million years ago. More questions with few answers. The computer may be able to extrapolate the data and find a human link to this planet. Wow – would that be awesome – will transmit all data to NASA tomorrow. Tomorrow we all will rover south again in search of more clues – everything seems to be.

DAY 8: Adam suggests they use the Rover-Lift to take the alien craft back to the ship and examine in detail – Robert, "Great idea Adam – let's do it!" They gently move it into the rover and take it back. Still no signs of birds or more carnivores. Strange. At the ship they unload the craft to the Med-Lab for computer analization. This might take a while – this new computer can do DNA analyzing with no blood or any secretions and just bones and the suits they wear. The family takes a long rest and a meal – they want real meat! Everyone takes a nap – it is early evening – sun is setting – a beautiful site – no moons on the planets. That's strange too! Many new things about this planet make no sense. Tomorrow Robert and Adam will seek out a herbivore (small) for dinner tomorrow night and hopefully celebrate finding out who and what these aliens are! Everyone is tired from that day so on Day 9, Robert and Adam head south looking for herds of herbivores – which they still haven't named! They will look closely and find a dinosaur from Earth that looks similar. Good luck – 30-40 tiger-size herbivores are grazing in front of them – they will use the rovers plasma gun turret tracking to kill one and take it back – all of a sudden – they scatter as a large carnivore breaks into the pack. Robert uses the turret to kill one about a mile away and in the southern hemisphere. That is where we will find the answers. These cave dwellers always either didn't breathe oxygen or something else in the atmosphere killed them long ago. We will find out this week.

DAY 10: Our rover is such a pleasure to drive (mostly Adam) rugged and dependable. We are halfway to the pole now and the valleys are so beautiful – some clouds now – but no storms or earthquakes anywhere. That one meteor shower of very small rock grains – I think they just are ignored by the animals. They have tough exteriors – but quite tasty inside. Lindy is rattling off a lot of checklists and GPS coordinates – our 2 satellites cover the whole planet quite well. I sent a transmission to NASA early. Should get word when we return to the ship later. Some larger hills and mountains appear and some herbivores are grazing – there are thousands of them here – we decided to name them Lindoceras for Lindy – she really loves seeing those gentle creatures! Maybe more caves or ship crash remains. We are excited – never been this far south. Clouds intensify and whamo – another short burst of meteors – they are actually soft and no threat – lost about 10 minutes and the Lindoceras just ignore them! We are so happy with the beauty and bounty of our new home! We could live here a long time if necessary – no other humans of-course. The computer still works non-stop on solving the mystery of our ancient alien friends – they are definitely bi-peds and human looking and of course intelligent to land here and have inter-galactic space travel. We are all very healthy – nothing in the atmosphere is caustic to humans and now – thanks to Daisy – we know which plants to avoid contact with. Kristen and I know to keep the kids aware of danger – but let them be excited and exploring! Larger mountains ahead – we are 65°S latitude and the temp is still high 60's – very comfortable – we will need to find a pass thru these mountains! They are about 10-15,000 feet high - no snow or ice – then Adam yells – look at that peak – it appears something ripped off the top of it. We must investigate the rover– they then manoeuvre thru some boulders and we are next to the peak and see debris scattered ahead – it looks like another alien ship! As we get closer, it's a big one scattered over a mile or more. We decide to spread out and walk the debris field (carrying our pulse rifles, of course) – we disburse – "stay in visual contact with the rover at all times –" I tell the crew!

Kristen and I hit the middle of the debris field and Adam on one side, Daisy and Lindy on the other – pieces of unknown metal and instruments scattered everywhere – its like the American Desert southwest – dry – so little rust or decay and no vein. All of a sudden Adam finds a body in a suit. It's another alien humanoid biped. They look almost identical to us in size and shape – we will take everything back to the ship. This is getting fun – then another carnivore – a big one – about 8 ft long and 7 ft tall with fangs and claws – its approaching so I decide to stun it with my plasma rifle to see how it reacts and gain some respect from the beasts. Wham – right in the chest – it is stunned – falls over and then slowly moves and eyes us – you can tell – it doesn't want another shot like that – we may have gotten the respect we need, to not be taken as it's herbivores prey! Horray! We bring the rover over and load up all the debris. This is the greatest find on the planet yet. "Betty" will enjoy examining these!

Aliens found in crashed ship debris field

In this part of the galaxy, the sensors have detected that the entire land mass of the planet floats on an underground ocean of fresh water! This is almost impossible. How did it form and how deep is the water? It is a true paradise. All the fish must be underground – but why no birds move questions than answers – but they have only been here 10 days!

Day 11 – The new alien crew ship crashed here about 800,000 years ago, when man was just developing. Did we come from these alien creatures? It is quite possible. The computer has found our DNA to be very similar to these aliens. A whole new theory to consider. A comm with NASA tomorrow evening to let them know what we have. Everyone is very excited! With each day I see my family love this planet even more as Kristen and I do as well. We await NASA's response and go to sleep feeling proud of our day 10 finds. Everything is working well! The occasional asteroid storms are plotted – so we know when to be inside. They don't bother any of the animals. The carnivores stay away from us – we have the site vehicles and weapons they respect. Our telescope can see our home system; but not Earth very well. It's too small.

DAY 11: Comm from NASA – "Betty" plays it = NASA wants us to stay here and continue to discover and develop the planet. Intelligent aliens here – some survived – where did they go and come from? We will find out. Kristen and I have discussed another child – the first human born outside Earth we know of. The kids don't know – but Med-Lab will make it happen and safely.

We have many things to discuss and figure out but on Day 11 – we have accomplished a lot!

The future is up to us to shape – and we are all very excited – as is Earth! Life is good! Each night we can see over 1 million stars many hundreds of thousands of light years away. Will the aliens come back – that is our biggest question. We go to bed with great expectations of what each day will bring. We are now Earth's furthest and most advanced outpost. Mars is just a short hop away from Earth and only has a few habs – making no real progress – as we are!

EPILOGUE

The Graving family and all they know and don't know has been detected – NASA left the ultimate decision up to the crew and the 100% decided to stay on this amazing planet of beauty and danger. In only 2 weeks – they discovered all the southern hemisphere and most of the northern. Geologically speaking – this planet makes no sense! It has no tilt for seasons – which may be because of no moon – what life exists below that remains to be seen. The sun is the size and age of our sun and this planets atmosphere blocks all harmful radiation – humans don't age! Barring a catastrophe or comet impact, this family could live here forever. The Earth may never solve the hyperdrive problem and have to resort to other means. The crew – thanks to Daisy's sensor analysis – found this oasis in the sky! They have all the essential oxygen (not important!), Water – unlimited – and vegetation and a healthy meat source among the herbivores of the planet. Plenty to go around "Life is good" – says Robert and Kristen – we are happy here and not lonely – we have each other forever.

Family taking a break during the training

Robert

Kristen

Adam

Daisy

Lindy

"May you fare as well on your time travel adventure!"

AUTHOR BIOGRAPHY

Charles Vaden started his career with a mechanical engineering degree from Clemson University, joined the Marine Corps and serve 11 years as a Harrier pilot, then an engineer and quality control specialist for Link Flight Simulation. After 2 years there he was hired by FEDEX as a pilot, and joined the Air Force and Air national Guard flying F-16, serving a combat tour in Iraq, and also flying and working for NASA. He has published several fiction and non-fiction books and had considerable knowledge of space dynamics and spacecraft systems. He has extrapolated his current aerodynamic and space mechanics knowledge to bring us this fictional space family of what easily one day could come true; but as he is fond of saying many times; "If you can't exceed the speed of light, you aren't going anywhere!"